eyes only

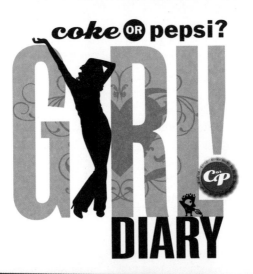

coke OR pepsi?
GIRL!
DIARY

WRITTEN AND DESIGNED BY

MICKEY AND CHERYL GILL

FINE print
PUBLISHING

Fine Print Publishing Company
P.O. Box 916401
Longwood, Florida 32971-6401

Created in the U.S.A. & Printed in China
This book is printed on acid-free paper.

ISBN 978-1-892951-48-9

2 3 5 7 9 10 8 6 4

coke-or-pepsi.com

All the thoughts,
dreams, and totally
random stuff of

name

year

Who says a diary has to be all princess-like, glittery, and full of blank pages?

GIRL! Diary is anything BUT!

Rock a poster all about yourself.
Rip out a page and send it to
your friend. Never forget those
super weird dreams.
Answer really personal
(and ridiculous) questions.
Scribble wildly on red hot mad
days. And no fears, there's
plenty of space to ink in all
the deets of your
anything-but-
average life.

your full name

how many other words
are in your name? List 'em.

what makes you smile?

leave a lipstick or lip gloss kiss here.

what makes you cry?

what are your fave days of the year?

tape some strands of your hair here.

IF YOU

1. could name a newly discovered planet, what would u call it?

_____

2. could make a wish come true for 1 friend, who would u pick

and what's the wish? _____

_____

3. were really famous, who would u like to hang out with?

_____

4. won a trip around the world for 5, which 4 people would

you take with u & y? _____

_____

_____

5. were guaranteed a position in any popular band, what band

would u choose and y? _____

_____

If your friends were dogs, what kinds would they be?

friend	dog
Yanni	Chawa

Think about
V
~~TO DO~~ LIST

L
I
S
T

everything
you Spend
most of your
time THINKING
about.

(if you're stumped, ask
your friends. they'll know.)

I'M OBSESSED WITH

_____

NOW,
Write the #1 thing you think about in the thought bubble.

What do u think about

○ Luv 'em! ○ Yuck!

1. If you could shrink one thing in your life, what would you choose? _____

_____

2. What one thing would you want to really, really super-size? _____

3. List everything you put ketchup on. _____

4. Something you do when no one's looking? _____

_____

5. If you could teleport anywhere for one hour, where would you go?

_____

_____

BF, BFF, Friend, Frenemy, Old Friend, New Friend, or Kinda Friend, Bud, Etc.

Friend...

1. who makes you LOL the most? _____

2. who makes you mad the most? Why? _____

3. who makes you sad the most? Why? _____

4. you miss? _____

5. you talk to every single day? _____

6. who is sometimes a bad influence on you? How? _____

7. who is always a good influence? How? _____

8. you'll know for life? _____

9. you would trade places with for 1 day? _____

10. with the best wardrobe? _____

11. you know the least about? _____

12. who is most different from you? _____

13. who is most like you? _____

14. who adults really like? _____

15. who is the most talented? What does he or she do? _____

16. with the biggest family? How many brothers & sisters? _____

17. with the most pets? How many? What are they? _____

18. who lives the farthest away? _____

19. you may never see again? _____

20. you dream about the most? _____

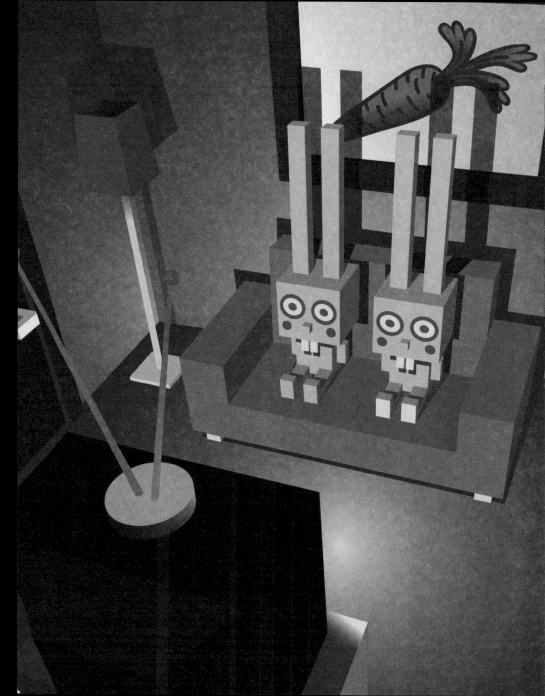

**TV show you and your friends
love to talk about?**

Fave TV show couple?

Absolute funniest ad running?

**Show you watch
(but wouldn't want your friends to know)?**

Re-run you love?

Funniest cartoon?

DRAMA!

What's the latest Drama in your life?

Turn it into a movie poster.

Draw a dramatic scene. (Just try.)

Give it a title.

Who are all the drama queens involved?

Who started it all?

Cool. Pick your musician to write the soundtrack.

Starring _____

_____

Directed by _____

Produced by _____

Music by _____

So, this is what I did differently,
and this is what happened ...

Make Today ALTERNATE UNIVERSE day.

Wear something you would normally never wear.
Get out of bed on the other side.
Eat something completely different for breakfast.
Take a new route between classes.
Talk to someone you've never talked to before.
Do the total opposite of

 what U usually do.

Draw your most worn-out pair of shoes. →

Y do U → (   )
wear them
so much?

How long have (   )   Farthest they've
u had them? ↵   ever traveled?

                                    ↘)
                              (

How does your
        mom feel about them?
        ↘
(   )

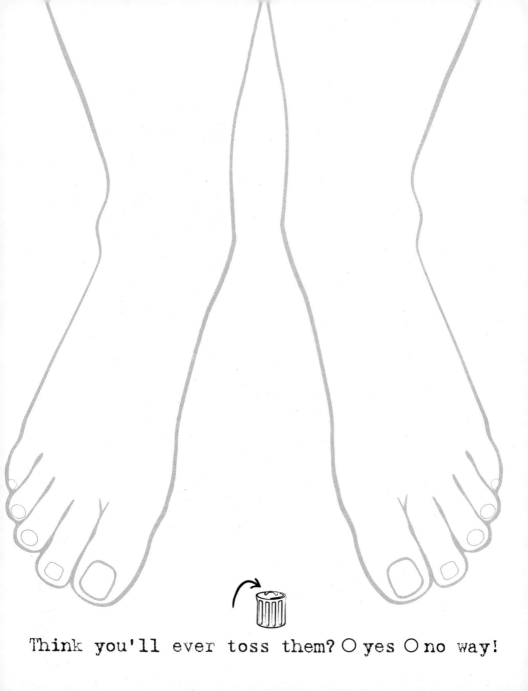

Think you'll ever toss them? ○ yes ○ no way!

What fictional character
(human or animal) from a book,
TV show, or movie would you love
to be friends with and why?

. . . .

. . . .

. . . .

. . . .

. . . .

. . . .

. . . .

Keep a dream log. Describe weird, awesome or scary ones you remember.

TODAY,

 BE

a little

 ~y.

(in a good way, of course.)

Find out some not-so-juicy nuggets of info about people in your world.

Ask a friend, classmate, teacher, etc. these random questions.

School coach: _____
<small>Name</small>

In ur opinion, what's the most fun pasta shape?

_____

Kid who sits to left of u in one of ur classes: _____
<small>Name</small>

When u get outta bed in the a.m., which foot hits the floor 1st?

_____

One of your teachers: _____
<small>Name</small>

What's something u bought because an ad made it look super cool?

_____

Best friend: _____
<small>Name</small>

Last thing you spit into a napkin cuz it was gross?

_____

Adult family member: _____
<small>Name</small>

What's ur best dance move? Ask for a demonstration.

Rate the move from 1-10, 10 being awesome. _____

What's 1 thing you're better @ than anyone else you know?

Write it here. ————

(Add your name to the plaque.)

gymnast • obnoxious laugher • doodler

chore avoider • basketball player • lipgloss artist

wait 'til the last minute studier

smoothie drinker • eye roller • secret keeper

Are you a GIRLY-GIRL?
or nah?

Last time you had a mani-pedi?

_____

Like your shoe color to match your outfit color?
O Yes O No

Is your bag bright & floral?
O Yes O No

How do you feel about PINK?
O Ugh! O OK O Luv it!

Prefer to hang with
O Girls O Guys?

SHE SAID

HOW DID YOU MEET
YOUR BEST GIRLFRIEND?
WHAT DID U LIKE
ABOUT HER?

SHE SAID

NOW, ASK HER IF
SHE REMEMBERS HOW YOU
MET & WHY YOU BECAME BF's.

DO
NOT
LABEL
ME.

CHECK OUT ALL THE LABELS
ON YOUR OUTFIT. DRAW THEM HERE.
(OR, PHOTOCOPY, CUT THEM OUT,
& TAPE THEM DOWN.)

1. Do you like hugging? ○ Yes ○ Not really.
Last person u hugged? _____

2. Who deserves a pie in the face? _____

_____

— 3. If you had a world audience for 5 minutes
what would you say to them? _____

_____

4. I've always wondered _____

_____.

5. Do you cry easily? ○ Yes ○ No.
Cry when ur super happy? ○ Huh? ○ Yep!

If you could be invisible today, what would you do?

Where would u go?

_____

_____

_____

_____

_____

_____

_____

Use only 1 word 2 describe today. Write it over & over again.

Use different fonts. write the word

Really Big.

Then, really small. Cut letters out from magazines and glue down. Write it, just using glue. Staple the word. Try lipstick. Paint with nail polish. Masking tape. Print. Write in cursive. Now, in a foreign language.

----

date

was

MAKES YOU THINK

Write down someone, something, some place, etc. you love in the star.

Then, think of 3 other things this word makes you think of and write those words in the connected bubbles.

Keep moving thru all the bubbles until they are filled.

Pretty cool - it's your mind network.

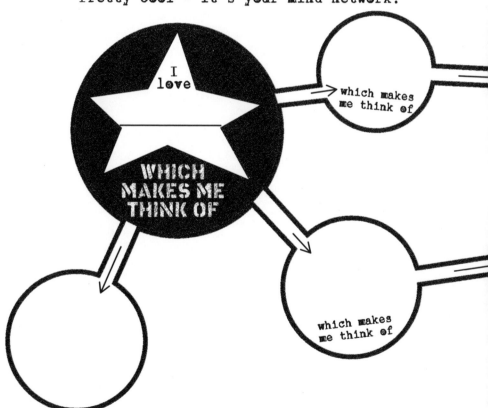

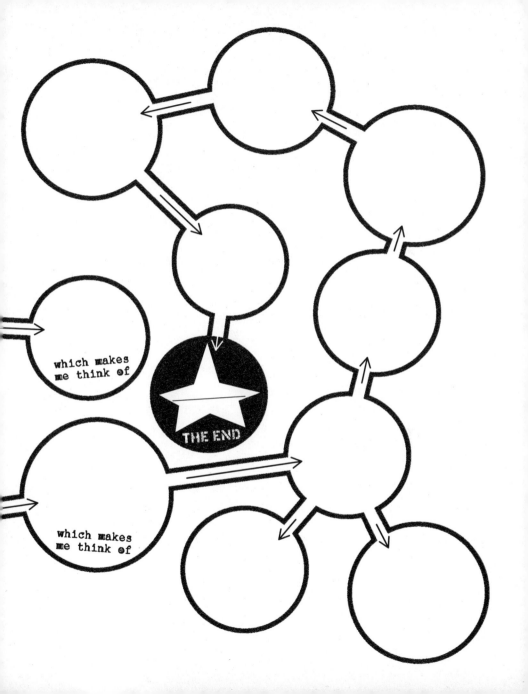

which makes
me think of

THE END

which makes
me think of

ROCK A POSTER STARRING YOU

MAKE SOME THINGS REALLY BIG AND OTHERS SMALL.
USE DIFFERENT FONTS. DRAW PICTURES.

WRITE —
YOUR FIRST NAME.
YOUR BIRTH DATE.
NAME OF YOUR SCHOOL.

2 FOODS YOU LOVE.
SOME OF YOUR FRIENDS' NAMES.
YOUR FAVE MOVIE.
A FEW LYRICS OF SONG YOU REALLY LIKE.

NOW, DRAW —
1 OF YOUR FRIENDS.
A PET OR ANIMAL YOU LOVE.
YOUR BEST DOODLES.

List all the reasons why you and your crush would be or ARE the perfect couple.

List all the reasons why you might not be. (Like he lives in Japan or your parents don't like him.)

- - - - - - - - - - - - - -   - - - - - - - - - - - - -

- - - - - - - - - - - - - -   - - - - - - - - - - - - -

- - - - - - - - - - - - - -   - - - - - - - - - - - - -

- - - - - - - - - - - - - -   - - - - - - - - - - - - -

- - - - - - - - - - - - - -   - - - - - - - - - - - - -

- - - - - - - - - - - - - -   - - - - - - - - - - - - -

- - - - - - - - - - - - - -   - - - - - - - - - - - - -

- - - - - - - - - - - - - -   - - - - - - - - - - - - -

- - - - - - - - - - - - - -   - - - - - - - - - - - - -

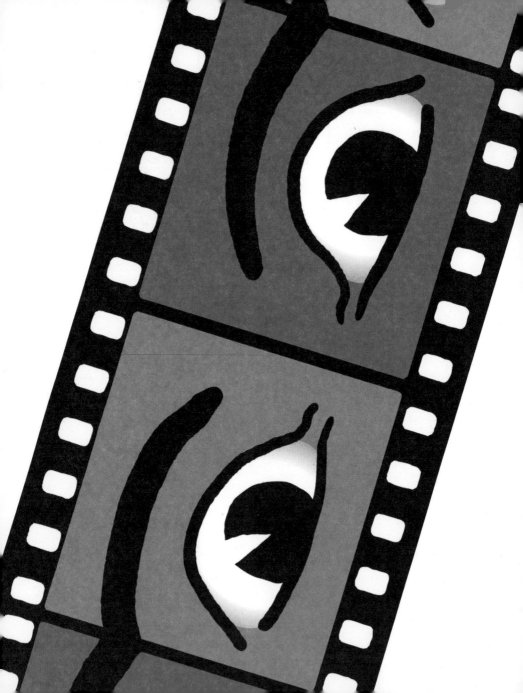

Last great movie you saw?

_____

Why'd you love it so much?

_____

Movie you've watched the most?

_____

How many times have you seen it? [ ]

Fave kind of flicks?

- ○ Sci-Fi
- ○ Romance
- ○ Horror
- ○ Documentary
- ○ Fantasy
- ○ Thriller
- ○ Comedy
- ○ Adventure
- ○ Animated

What do you refuse to do in front of people? _____

What are you AFRAID to do in public? _____

What do you LOVE to do in public? _____

Crowds ○ make me feel claustrophobic ○ are awesome!

What do you like to do alone? _____

What do you hate to do alone? _____

Do you like talking ○ one-on-one ○ with a group of people?

On a scale from 1-5, (5 being sweating-like-a-pig nervous), how nervous
are you before giving a presentation at school? 1   2   3   4   5

Describe your best public performance. _____

_____

Describe your worst public performance. _____

_____

HOW'S YOUR

DAY

DATE

○ AWESOME!

○ am in like ○ am in love ○ have a crush on

○ PRETTY GOOD

○ AWFUL!

Here's what's goin' on.

Write the letter, text, chat, & whatever that you'll never send.

"I love you." Or, "I can't believe you did that to me." All those things you want to tell someone ...
but you don't. Write it here.
Get it out of your system. Never send it.

To:

From:

What happened today, from worst to best?
(#5)   (#1)

5. _____

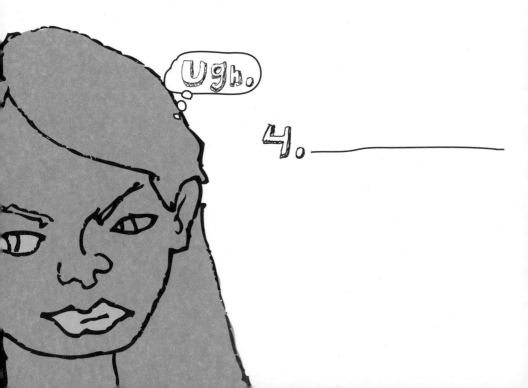

Ugh.

4. _____

3. _____

2. _____

U as a scientific study.

Chart your moods 4 one week.

scary!

dot
↓
Put a ● next to your mood for that day.
Connect the dots at the end of the week.

Day	totally excited	crazy good	happy	calm & cool	angry	grumpy	so sad
Saturday							
Friday							
Thursday							
Wednesday							
Tuesday							
Monday							
Sunday							

What's the scariest thing you've ever done OR that has happened to you?

_____

_____

_____

_____

_____

_____

_____

_____

Coolest thing about the bro(thers)? _____

_____

_____

Grossest thing? _____

the bro (thers)

_____

How r u like him/them? _____

_____

Last time one embarrassed you? _____

_____

the parents

Most awesome thing about Mom/Dad? _____

_____

_____

How r u like them? _____

_____

Whaddya luv about him/her? _____

_____

_____

How does ur best friend bug u? _____

_____

_____

Best time you've ever had 2gether? _____

_____

Maddest you've ever been @ her/them? _____

_____

_____

Nicest thing about the sis(ters)? _____

_____

_____

Look like sis(ters)? ◯ No ◯ Yes, we have the same _____

_____

You have the chance to meet a **Celebrity!**
Who would you pick?

Celeb name

Where would you like to meet ms./Mr. Celeb?

Who would you let tag along?

What would you wear?

List 5 things you would tell her/him about yourself.
1.
2.
3.
4.
5.

You can ask only 5 questions.
What would they be?
1.
2.
3.
4.
5.

This is your
**VIRTUAL
TREE.**
Carve messages
into it
with a pen.

"So-and-so
loves what's
his name."
"Hug a tree today."
Or write some
juicy deets
about your life.

No trees were hurt during this exercise.

is some-one reading your diary?

then turn the page.

① pull this sprea

② cut messages

③ fold and place

- - - - - - - - - -

SNOOPE

I know who you are, & I kn

- - - - - - - - - -

KEEP

out of your diary.

t along dotted lines.

nywhere in diary.

- - - - - - - - - - -

R ALERT!

v what you've been doing.

- - - - - - - - - - -

OUT!

think some- one found your diary

← then turn the page.

HERE IS A WORD GAME. IT'S SUPER REVEALING!

Write down the first word, sentence, or entire story that comes to mind when you see the words...

SLEEPING BAG

PURPLE

VAMPIRE

SNEAKERS

DAISIES

WHAT KIND OF MUSIC DO YOU LISTEN 2?
WHO R YOUR FAVORITE BANDS OR SINGERS?
WHAT EXACTLY DO YOU LIKE ABOUT THEM?

_____

_____

_____

_____

_____

_____

_____

_____

1. Copy your last text message or IM with a friend here.

2. If u were a geometric shape, what would u b?

_____

3. R u the ○ first ○ last to raise your hand? y? _____

4. What gives you the creeps?

_____

5. R u a whiner? ○ No ○ Yes, I whine a lot about_____.

WE do

List everything you and your parents disagree about.

Your viewpoint

- - - - - - - - - - - - - -

- - - - - - - - - - - - - -

- - - - - - - - - - - - - -

- - - - - - - - - - - - - -

- - - - - - - - - - - - - -

- - - - - - - - - - - - - -

- - - - - - - - - - - - - -

- - - - - - - - - - - - - -

n't see.

Their viewpoint

- - - - - - - - - - - - - - - -

- - - - - - - - - - - - - - - -

- - - - - - - - - - - - - - - -

- -

- -

- -

- -

- -

Write about your day from beginning to end, without using any punctuation. Don't tell your English teacher. ☝ Oh yeah, write within the path. ↘

start

RIP THESE PAGES OUT. »

TAKE THEM WITH YOU.

SOUNDS LIKE A PERSONAL PROBLEM.

TAPE THEM UP↑.

SEND THEM OFF.

NO! WAY!

then collect them and stash 'em in your diary pocket.

PROTECTED AREA PLEASE KEEP OUT

HUH? seriously?

Sneak away some-where while @ school-

to a quiet corner between classes
or go 2 the bathroom or something.

WHAT TIME IS IT?

_____ , _____
Day   Date

where are YOU?

Describe your
surroundings.

- -

- -

- -

Now, take something AWAY (without stealing of course.)

Look for a small found object and tape it here.

YOU as ART

1. Tear this page out, flip over, and tape to a wall.

2. Turn off lights.

3. Ask a friend to shine a light on blank sheet.

4. Turn sideways and put your face against sheet.
   Trace your shadow profile.

5. Completely fill in your profile with words
   that describe u. Ask your friend for help.

PASS THIS NOTE
(You know, instead of texting, chatting, etc. Tell your friend(s) about your day... with pen & paper. Fold it up & pass it back & forth. Crazy, right?)

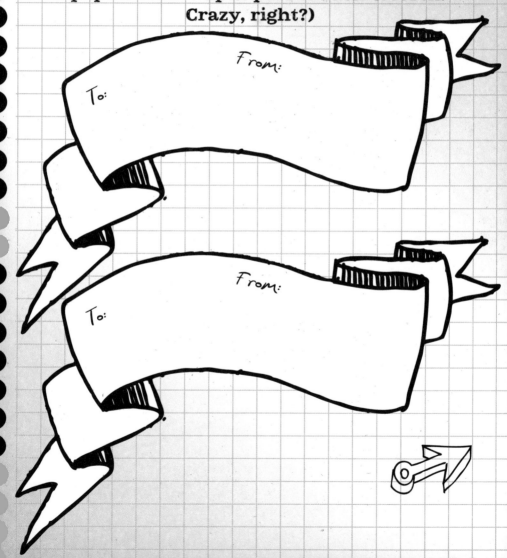

From:

To:

From:

To:

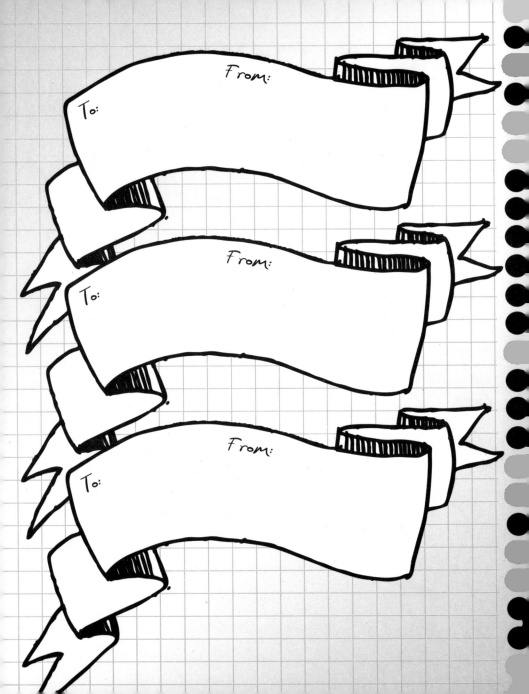

Save this for a really

MAD

day.

What r u angry about?

Now poke out all the dots above.
If that doesn't help, scribble all over the paper.

Write a really short letter to someone.
Send it in the regular mail – a.k.a. mail.

Dear _____,   _____
                                    Date

Write a letter to me on the other side of this.
Mail back to me.

Dear _____, _____
Date

TAKE THIS
SOMEWHERE
OTHER THAN SCHOOL.

WHERE ARE YOU?

{ }

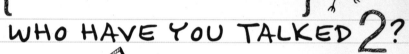

WHO HAVE YOU TALKED 2?

{ }

Day of the week { }

DATE {

QUICK!

LIST SHORT
DETAILS
OF YOUR DAY
SO FAR.

 Best thing about day?

Worst thing?

DRAW YOUR LUNCH ➊ THEN ➋

who'd you eat with?

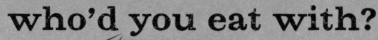

what did you talk about?

Cut this bracelet out.

Wrap around your wrist and tape.
(cut in 2 strips if u need a longer bracelet.)

Wear it all day. Write your Diary entry on it.

Dear Diary,

_____
date

Flip your bracelet over and use it for another day. :)

Dear Diary,

_____ date

MY TOTALLY RANDOM DAY

KEEP YOUR DIARY WITH YOU FOR ONE ENTIRE DAY.
DESCRIBE WHAT'S GOIN' ON @

6:31 AM

11:43 AM

3:03 PM

7:59 PM

11:11 PM

PoUr

all the contEnts of
your hearT, soul, and mind out heRe.

Write, stick thiNgs doWn,
do whateVer on thesE pages.

write here

write here

ah-chi-wow-wah!

write here

Looking for your
diary Key?

write here

write here

write here

write here

_____

_____

_____

_____

_____

_____

_____

_____

_____

_____

_____

_____

Ooo... that really happened?

whate

cut oUt PhOtos.
TapE heRE.

wriTe caPtiOns
for PiCs.

CHECKOU

coke-or-pepsi.com
for more
**books,
quizzes**
& c-or-p
stuff!